Fruits, Roots, and Fungi

Plants We Eat

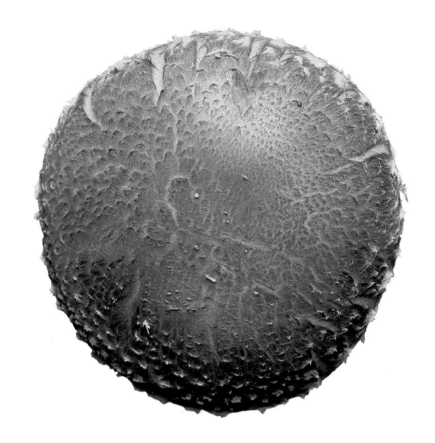

text and photos by Isamu Sekido

 Lerner Publications Company • Minneapolis

Series Editor: Susan Breckner Rose

This edition first published 1993
by Lerner Publications Company.
Originally published 1984 in Japanese under the title
Atete Goran by Kaisei-Sha Publishing Co., Ltd.

English translation rights arranged with Kaisei-Sha
Publishing Co., Ltd. through Japan Foreign-Rights Centre.

Library of Congress Cataloging-in-Publication Data

Sekido, Isamu, 1946-
    [Atete goran. English]
    Fruit, roots, and fungi : plants we eat / text and photos
by Isamu Sekido.
        p.   cm.
    Summary: Depicts and discusses edible parts of
plants, challenging the reader to identify them from
the photographs.
    ISBN 0-8225-2902-5
    1. Plants, Edible–Juvenile literature. 2. Vegetables–
Juvenile literature. 3. Fungi, Edible–Juvenile literature.
[1. Plants, Edible. 2. Vegetables.] I. Title.
QK98.5.AIS4513   1993
581.6′32–dc20   92-19958
                                               CIP
                                                AC

Manufactured in the United States of America

1   2   3   4   5   6   98   97   96   95   94   93

Much of the food we eat comes from plants. Most of the plants we eat are flowering plants. Flowering plants have roots, stems, leaves, flowers, and seeds. The fruit is the part of a flowering plant that surrounds the seeds.

This looks more like a road map than something we eat. But behind these crisscrossing lines is a soft, sweet fruit. Do you know what this fruit is? ▶

MELON

These lines are on the outside, or **rind,** of the fruit of a melon. When a melon is cut open, you can see the soft, juicy **pulp** surrounding the seeds. The rind and the pulp both protect the seeds. The part of the melon plant that we eat is the juicy pulp of the fruit.

In the spring, the melon plant has flowers (1).

The flower petals **wither,** and the part of the flower that is left begins to grow into a fruit (2).

As the fruit grows larger (3-5), the rind starts to harden and becomes covered with cracks (6-7).

When the fruit is ripe (8), it starts to separate from the stem. It is then ready to be picked and eaten.

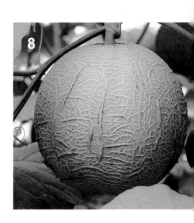

Melon plants have long **vines.** Vines are the soft stems of plants that climb up fences or creep along the ground. Melon plants spread their vines in all directions, which helps them produce more fruit. In this melon field, the plants have attached themselves to a fence using their finger-like **tendrils.** Tendrils curl around whatever is near them to help support the vines. These melons are not quite ripe. ■

This looks like the rind of a fruit. This fruit is usually called a vegetable. But what is the cork-like button in the middle? ▶

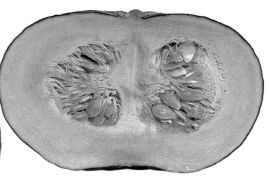

SQUASH

This is a squash. Although we often call it a **vegetable,** a squash is actually a fruit—its golden pulp surrounds large, flat seeds.

Like the melon, the part of the squash that we eat is the pulp surrounding the seeds. The fruit of the squash plant grows the same way that a melon does. When the flower withers, the fruit starts to grow. The button on top of the fruit is where the squash was attached to the stem. ■

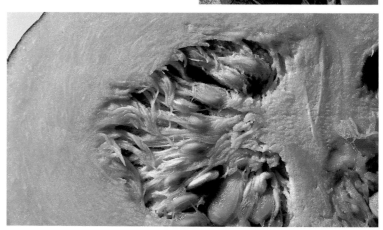

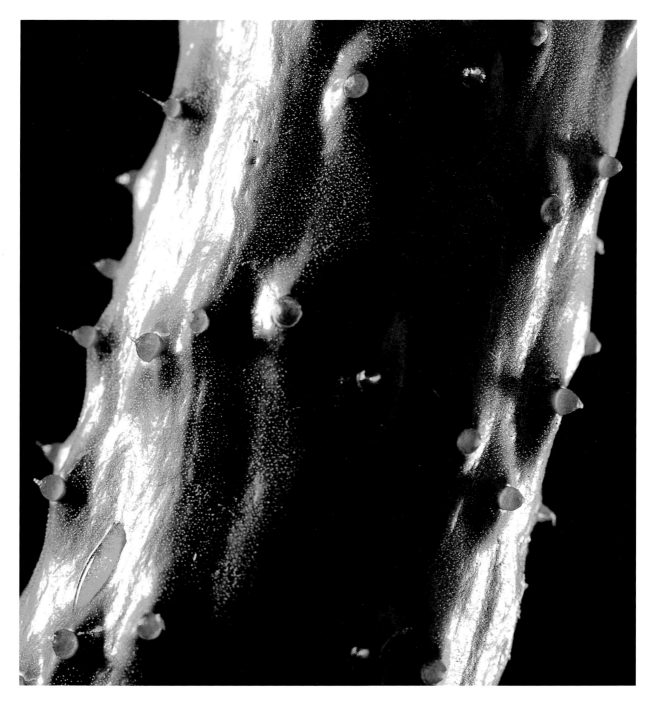

This mysterious-looking green thing is a fruit too. Like melons and squashes, it grows on a vine. Can you guess what this green thing is? ▶

CUCUMBER

A cucumber is another fruit. Cucumbers grow on vines that twine their tendrils around whatever object is closest to them. As the flower withers (*left*), the fruit (*below left*) begins to grow. Cucumber leaves (*right*) look similar to squash and melon leaves. This is because all three plants are in the same family.

The withered petals of the flower are still attached to this sliced-open cucumber (*below right*). Inside the cucumber are the seeds. ■

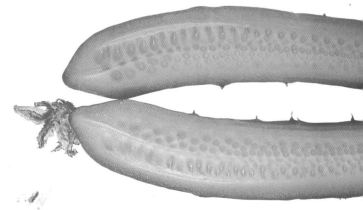

10

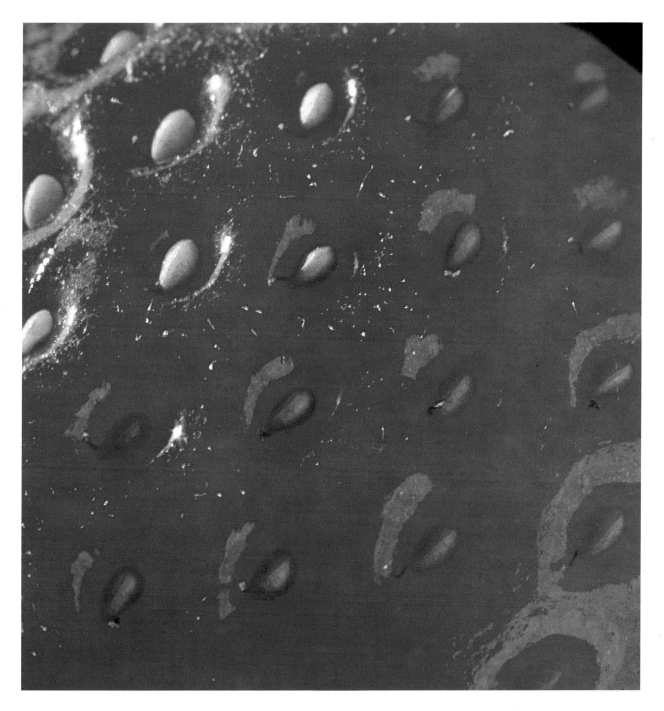

We eat this sweet, red fruit in slices on cereal, pancakes, ice cream, and cakes. We also make jam or jelly from it. What is this sweet, red fruit? ▶

STRAWBERRY

Each strawberry plant produces white, sweet-smelling flowers. The flower petals fall off, and a small, green, fleshy lump begins to grow where the flower once was. This lump is covered with straw-colored flecks that look like seeds. Each fleck is really a separate fruit that contains a seed. Together all of these separate fruits make up a **compound fruit.** So a strawberry is a compound fruit. As a strawberry ripens, it turns from green to red and grows bigger and softer. ■

You can easily see why this is a fruit. The light brown seeds are surrounded by crunchy, green pulp. Is this usually called a fruit or a vegetable? ▶

 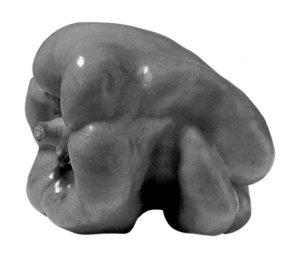

BELL PEPPER

A pepper flower (*left*) becomes a pepper fruit. Inside the fruit are the seeds (*lower left*). Often, peppers are picked off the plant and eaten when they are still green (*below*).

But if they are left on the plant, most peppers will turn red, and some will turn yellow, purple, or orange. ■

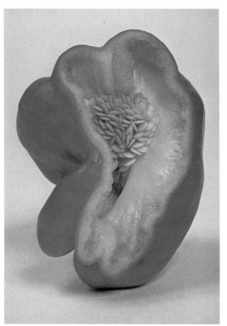 

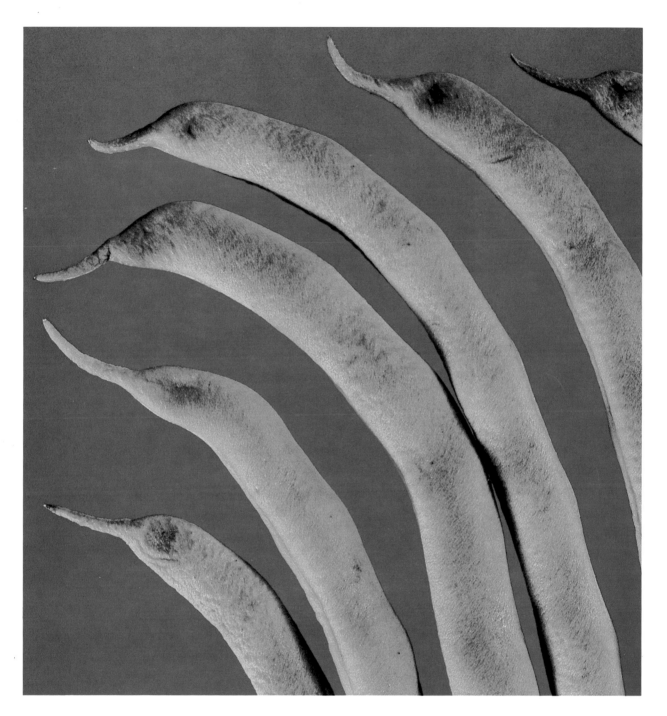

These long, green fruits contain the seeds of a plant that flowered earlier. Sometimes we eat the whole fruit. Other times we eat only the seeds. What are these long fruits? ▶

BEAN

These are beans. Some bean plants are bushy (*below left*), some are climbing vines (*below right*). Beans from both these plants are usually picked when the seeds can be felt through the skin, but before the beans have dried. ■

These rounded arches are the part of a plant that we eat, but the arches don't surround any seeds. Instead, they make up what is called a bulb. Do you know what this bulb is? ▶

ONION

Onion bulbs are the thicker and rounder base of onion leaves. The bulbs grow partially underground. They store food for the rest of the onion plant. The top part of the leaves are long and thin. After the onion flower (*right*) dries, the thin leaves also wither, and the onion bulb is ready to be picked (*below*). ■

What are these crinkly, curly lines? They could be leaves, but leaves are usually green, not red. Do you know what part of a plant this is? ▶

RED CABBAGE

The part of a cabbage that we eat is layer upon layer of leaves. The leaves grow close together into a tightly formed ball, or head (*right*). If a head of cabbage is not picked soon enough, or if the weather gets too hot, the inside leaves will grow faster than the outside leaves. The head will crack and split open. Then a stalk will grow out of the middle of the cabbage and produce flowers (*lower right*). ■

These ridges are part of a plant that never flowers and does not make seeds. It does not even have leaves. But it is a plant that we eat. What is this plant? ▶

MUSHROOM

A mushroom is a **fungus.** Most of the mushroom plant is a web of thread-like roots called **mycelium.** The mycelium grows underground or under the bark of a tree. The part of the mushroom that grows above ground is called a **fruiting body.** The fruiting body produces tiny **spores.** Spores are smaller and simpler than seeds, but like seeds, they grow into new plants. Many mushrooms are poisonous, but this shiitake mushroom is **edible.** It is safe and good to eat! ■

We eat different parts of many kinds of plants. An everyday salad could include all the parts of flowering plants–roots, leaves, stems, and fruits–and a fungus too. A carrot is a root. Lettuce is a leaf. Celery is a stem. A tomato is a fruit. And a mushroom is the fruiting body of a fungus. As you think of other plants we eat, can you figure out what part of the plant they are?

GLOSSARY

compound fruit: a cluster of seed-bearing fruitlets that make up a complete fruit

edible: fit to be eaten

fruiting body: the part of the mushroom that grows above ground and produces spores

fungus: a plant that has no leaves, flowers, or green color. Mildews, molds, yeasts, and mushrooms are forms of fungus.

mycelium: the web of thread-like roots of a mushroom

pulp: the soft, juicy part of a fruit

rind: the hard or firm outer layer of a fruit

spore: the tiny seed produced by fungi that can grow into a new fungus

tendril: a small, curly stem that holds up a climbing plant by coiling around something

vegetable: a plant that is grown for food and only lives for one growing season. We eat the roots, stems, leaves, and fruits of vegetables.

vine: a plant with a long, thin stem that grows along the ground or climbs up fences

wither: to dry up or shrivel